The Protectors

A Novelette

B. Love

Prolific Pen Pusher

Preface

Please note: These are different timeframes. The weddings/pregnancies are not congruent since the ladies were pregnant at different times. These are update chapters only. No full plots. Enjoy.

1

Asylum
September
     I thought Doe was irresistible to me before, but watching her grow my baby in her womb made it impossible for me to keep my hands off her. The fact that she was risking her health and life, putting a lot of things on hold to ensure she had a safe and healthy pregnancy and delivery, made me love and respect her even more. I was truly grateful to God and appreciative even more for my woman, women in general, and there wasn't a damn thing I wouldn't do for her.

On top of her carrying my child, I loved the relationship she'd developed with True. Though she stressed she wasn't trying to be a second mother or replacement for Sierra, my sweetheart took care of True and considered her as if she was her own.

A perfect example of that was how today she'd put together a special day for us and True, to make sure she understood the baby we were about to have wasn't going to replace her. It hadn't crossed my mind to have a conversation like this with True, because I knew that was the case, but the way she considered my baby girl and intentionally wanted to validate her place in our lives before the new baby came had me ready to serve her at her feet.

Doe obsessed over things, wanting them to be perfect, so it didn't surprise me to find her in the dining room, looking over the setup Swayde had created. Swayde had a tea bar in Jasper Lane that was dope as hell. She didn't usually travel for parties, but she made an exception for Doe... and for the amount of money I offered her to do this for my babies. Doe wanted to have a tea party with True. She had hot water stations and several different kinds of tea on a custom menu to choose from, along with finger sandwiches and pastries that complemented each tea.

The shit was cute as hell, I couldn't lie, and I knew True would love it.

Walking over to Doe, I stood behind her and lifted her belly. Immediately, her body relaxed against me.

"Mm," she moaned before giggling as I held her belly up and gently rocked her from side to side. "How'd you know this was just what I needed?"

"Just a guess."

I placed a kiss to her neck, loving how her giggles sounded. I wanted to do everything in my power to keep her comfortable while she carried my son. It wasn't lost on me that with her being a first-time mom, there were changes within her body she'd been experiencing and how it might sometimes be painful or uncomfortable, and I wanted to do whatever I could to alleviate that.

"Thank you, babe. I can't describe how good it feels to be weightless... even if for just a few seconds."

"Well... our son will be here soon. Then you'll have your body back to yourself."

"And I cannot *wait*. I don't mind sharing it with him as long as I need to, but Mama is ready for him to come *out*."

That made me chuckle. He was due in three weeks, and we'd been counting down for different reasons.

"We need to decide on a name."

She turned in my arms. "I know you don't want him to be a junior."

My head shook. "Nah, I want him to carve his own path. I'll guide him, but I want him to be his own man."

"That's fair. Well, we still have a little time. Nothing has really resonated with me yet."

"Maybe we should just wait until he's here. Look at him. See what comes to us."

Her arms wrapped around my neck as she smiled. "I love the sound of that. That's actually perfect, Sy."

"Good."

Lowering my lips to hers, I kissed her until the doorbell rang. In no rush, I lowered my hands to her ass, wishing I could pull her closer, but Baby Boy was in the damn way. Doe chuckled as she pulled away.

"I feel like I can't get close enough to you," I muttered.

"Clearly. Three more weeks."

"Three more weeks," I repeated before heading toward the door. I didn't really feel like dealing with Sierra's ass, but since I wanted to stay behind in case Swayde and Doe needed my help with anything, I asked Sierra to drop True off.

Sierra had gotten a bit more stable over the last several months. She was working and had a three-bedroom apartment that was by her parents' home. Our schedule was split, so she had True two weeks out of the month, and so did I. We hadn't heard from Bobby, which I was grateful for. A part of me thought one day he'd regret signing over his rights, but that hadn't been the case.

I wouldn't say Sierra and I had any kind of relationship. We only talked about True. She asked about Doe and the baby from time to time, but I wasn't comfortable sharing any details about my life with her. I was willing to deal with her on behalf of True, but I'd never forget that stunt she pulled, and it had permanently changed the way I handled her.

"Hey, Daddy." True greeted me with a wide grin.

"Hey, baby girl," I replied, giving her a hug and kissing the top of her head. "Why didn't you use the code to let yourself in?"

"Mama said you and Ms. Doe might've been in here doing grown folks' stuff and that we needed to knock since you didn't answer the phone."

With a chuckle, I acknowledged Sierra with a bob of my head. "I 'preciate the consideration. I just didn't have my phone, though."

Sierra nodded and twiddled her thumbs. "Well... I guess I'll see you in two weeks, True, but I'll talk to you tomorrow."

"Okay, Mama. Bye!"

True gave Sierra a hug before heading down the hall in search of her friend. After I closed up behind Sierra, I led True to where Doe was waiting for us in the dining room. She was as excited by what Doe had done as I thought she would be. I made it clear this was Doe's idea because I wanted to make sure she knew Doe had her on her heart and mind.

Once we all had our tea and pastries, we got comfortable at the table.

"Doe and I want to talk to you to make sure you understand things might change a little around the house when

4

the baby gets here, but it won't change our love for you or our priority of you," I started. "You're still my princess, and us having a baby doesn't change that."

"How are you feeling about the new baby?" Doe asked.

True finished chewing her strawberry and cucumber sandwich before looking from me to Doe.

"At first I was a little sad," she admitted. "Well, I was happy but sad too."

"Why?" I asked.

"Because I didn't want you to not be my daddy anymore since you had your own baby."

That shit broke my fucking heart. It made me even more grateful that Doe wanted to have this conversation because it never crossed my mind that True would feel this way.

"Baby girl, whether you're my biological daughter or not, you'll *always* be my baby. That's why I'm adopting you."

"I know," she replied with a smile. "Mama reminded me of that. And she told me this baby is still going to be my little brother, even though he didn't come from her, because you're still going to be my daddy. So that made me excited about it because she said she's not going to have any more kids."

Doe and I laughed.

"If you ever feel sad or angry, you know you can come to us, right?" Doe confirmed.

"Yes, ma'am. I just didn't want to make either of you mad. But I'm okay with the new baby. I promise. I can't wait until he gets here."

"Well, we're gonna need your help with him," I told her. "You ready to change some diapers?"

"Ew! I'll do anything *but* that!" Her scowl caused Doe to release a hoot of laughter.

"Come on now, princess. How you not gon' change ya lil brother diapers?" I asked.

"Unh uh." Her head shook and face covered with disgust at just the thought, and I could no longer hold my laugh in. "I'll feed him, but I'm not changing no diapers."

We continued to commune well into the evening. I made the mental note to schedule a day out of the week to spend with my princess after the baby got here, where it was just us, to make sure she never questioned her priority in my life. I also made the mental note to call Sierra and thank her for what she'd said to True.

It seemed she helped her and didn't bother telling me, which let me know her intentions were pure. Sierra had a track record of being selfish and spiteful, and I was grateful she allowed that to remain a pure moment where she did what was best for our daughter.

Maybe there was hope for her yet.

2

D auterive

WHEN I AGREED TO A SPA DAY WITH MY SISTER, Dallas, I wasn't expecting it to end with us seeing Sierra on our way to lunch. I wouldn't say Sierra and I had a bad relationship, but we didn't have a good one either. We were cordial and respected each other. She'd done too much for me to ever fake the funk with her though.

It was still fresh that she'd lied about there being a possibility that Asylum was True's father. Even though we found our way back to each other, it still hurt that we parted ways almost fourteen years ago because of her lie. I had my man and knew nothing or no one would ever come between us, but still. That wasn't some shit I could just get over overnight.

And on top of what she did years ago, she did that flawed ass disappearing act. That didn't just hurt True; it hurt Asylum as well. She hurt two people who I loved and cared about because she was so self-absorbed and obsessed with a man who was never hers to begin with. I wasn't holding those things against her, but they definitely made me not like her as a person. I could respect that she'd apologized and tried to make amends, but that wasn't good enough for me. My fear was that, at a different time in the future, something could happen to make her respond like that again. She was the kind of person I'd never fully be able to trust.

Good thing was, it didn't matter. If she did leave True again, Sy and I were going to make sure she was taken care of.

"Can we talk?" Sierra asked, standing in front of me.

We were in the waiting area at a new restaurant that Dallas wanted to try. From the full tables, I would assume they were going to be good and worth the wait. It was a brunch buffet style restaurant, which was the first of its kind in the city.

"You can sit down and talk," I offered, moving my purse from next to me on the bench. I didn't really want to talk to her, but I would listen to what she had to say.

"True told me about the tea party. That was really sweet."

Nodding, I gave a small smile as Dallas stared at us. It wasn't funny, but the way my sister was ready to pop off tickled me.

"Dallas, will you see if they'll let you get me some water?"

Her eyes rolled as she stood and gave us some privacy, making me laugh.

"She looked like she was ready for me to say the wrong

8

thing so she could hit me," Sierra said with a chuckle and shook her head.

"That, she was."

"I take it that's because she knows about what happened years ago?"

"Yeah, and she knows about your disappearing act too."

With a sigh, Sierra sat back and leaned against the wall. "You don't like me... do you?"

"No, I don't. Would you like me if the roles were reversed?"

She sighed and squeezed the back of her neck. "I know me saying I'm sorry and that I'm not that same person anymore might not mean anything to you, but it's the truth. I spent so much time trying to keep a man that wasn't meant to be mine, and I hated what that did to me. The person it turned me into."

"You can't blame Sy for you lying about the paternity of your child."

"I'm not blaming him." She pulled in a deep breath. "I'm just saying, I did things I shouldn't have done to keep him. But I'm not on that type of time anymore. I know we'll never be friends, but I wanted to thank you for treating my daughter well and not holding what I've done over the years against her."

That softened me toward her—a little.

"I would never do that. True's the sweetest little girl. She got some fire in her though." We smiled. "You are doing good with her. Minus you temporarily abandoning her, you're raising a good child."

"Thank you. Um... I told Sy this, but... if the two of you ever need anything with the baby, he can always come over with True. She asked me if he could have our empty room." That made us both laugh. "I told her I doubt if y'all would trust me with him, but he will always have a place in our home as True's little brother."

"She told us that you assured her that she would always . be Sy's baby. Thank you for that."

"You don't have to thank me for that. It was the truth."

"Huh." Dallas extended a glass of water in my direction and kept her eyes on Sierra.

With a chuckle, Sierra stood as I accepted the water.

"Thank you, SiSi," I said, appreciating her stopping to try and develop more peace between us.

"No problem. You ladies enjoy your brunch."

"You as well," I replied as she walked away.

Dallas sucked her teeth, and I pinched her thigh as I laughed.

"Ow! Why you pinch me?"

"Why you mugging that lady like that?"

"Because I owe her an ass whupping for what she did to you, my brother, and my niece."

My eyes rolled as I shook my head. "You gon' have to learn to be soft in the face when she's around. I really don't think she's leaving again, so we have to get used to her."

"*You* have to get used to her. I ain't got to get used to *shit*."

With a chuckle, I crossed my arms over my chest. This girl was impossible, but I loved her for it. Sierra wasn't my favorite person in the world, but maybe there was hope for her yet.

3

Dauterive
October

I'D WAITED TOO LATE TO FLY FOR MY BABYMOON. WITH my due date being one week away, any travel we did would have to be done in a car. I didn't want to drive too far and be uncomfortable, so Asylum and I decided on Rose Valley Hills. It was only three hours away. I wasn't expecting much to be available to do in the beach town since it was fall, but we ended up having a lot of options.

I think my favorite thing that we'd done so far was the gondola ride that led us to a small studio where we were able to create our own candles, bouquets, and clay molds. We did a mold of my belly that would be shipped to us in a few weeks, and I couldn't wait to get it. We also had a mold casted of our hands intertwined. It was probably the most hands-on creative date I'd ever had, and I was glad it was with my fiancé. I loved that even after all these years, Sy and I were still able to have firsts together.

When we made it back to our hotel suite, I was in for the surprise of my life. I'd mentioned to him how the spa Dallas and I went to were unable to accommodate me for a massage because they were so busy, which was okay. I understood there was only one woman on staff who was trained to do it, and she was booked. To see that he'd booked a masseuse, who was ready and waiting to give me a full body massage, made me cry.

The ambiance was set with relaxing music and dim lighting, and he had a tray of fruit for me to nibble on too. For ninety minutes, I was in absolute heaven, and I couldn't wait for the masseuse to leave so I could thank him for it.

As soon as he closed the door behind Taylor, I was on him. He laughed as I kissed his lips and unbuckled his jeans.

"Doe..."

"Hmm?"

"What you doing?"

"It's not obvious?"

Laughing, Asylum took my hands into his. "Yeah, but I'm just surprised."

Removing my hand from his, I cupped his dick through his jeans. "You're hard too."

"You know all it takes for that to happen is one touch from you."

I smiled with one side of my mouth before connecting my lips with his. He helped me undress him. Since I was in undies under a cotton robe, it didn't take much for him to remove the robe. I squealed when he picked me up and carried me to bed.

"You sure?" he checked, kissing down my chest.

"Yes, babe. I'm sure."

Kisses and touches led to him entering me while I lay on my side. He was so gentle and careful. So slow and precise. I felt every inch of every stroke he filled me with. His hand moved from my stomach to my neck. Holding me in place, he alternated between kissing my neck, cheek, and lips.

"Oh my God," I moaned, speech slurred. The climax wasn't quick, but it was hard and intense. My entire body trembled and seized, and he continued to stroke me. My whimpers mixed with his moans as I gripped the back of his thigh.

"Damn, bae." He panted against my ear. Between the huskiness of his voice and the feel of his dick jerking inside of me, I shuddered.

Sitting up, Asylum tilted me slightly. I was still on my side but a little more on my back. He was conscious of my comfort—anchoring me and keeping me from being too flat. He held my thigh and belly as he filled me with long, medium-paced strokes. They were soft and careful, which somehow made me feel them more than the hard and deep strokes he'd been giving me before I got bigger.

When his hand moved from my belly to my clit, curses began to pour from my mouth.

"I luh this pussy," he moaned before biting down on his bottom lip. "Don't ever stop giving me this shit."

"Yes, Sy." Gripping his wrist, I tried to keep my eyes on his, but it felt so good I couldn't help but close them as he continued to make love to me. "Just like that, babe. Please, please don't stop."

"I got you, sweetheart. Cum as much as you want on this dick."

He rested my leg against his chest, lengthening his strokes.

I came three more times before he was completely empty, and I was too tired to do anything but sleep with a smile on my face and pure joy in my heart.

4

A sylum

"WHAT ELSE DO YOU HAVE UP YOUR SLEEVE, SIR?" DOE asked me skeptically.

We were on day four of the babymoon and had three days left. I had not one complaint about our time in Rose Valley Hills. It allowed us to detach from everything and everyone and focus on each other. Not only that, but we also needed the rest.

"I want it to be a surprise," I told her as I closed the door behind her. We'd just arrived at the botanic garden owned by herbalist Mali Tyson, and I was a bit nervous. Not because I felt like she would say no to my plan, but because of what it would mean if she said yes.

"Well, I need to pee. So can you find me a bathroom before the surprise?"

Chuckling, I checked the map that was a few feet in

front of the door, being sure to keep her away from the exhibit that had been reserved for just us. I walked her to the bathroom, and once she was done handling her business, we went inside. She was so busy trusting my lead that she didn't notice we didn't pay to get in. The whole time we walked, she held my hand and hummed in her own little world. I loved that she felt so safe with me.

At the sight of us, Mali's assistant gasped. She looked more like a teacher than anything else with her pantsuit, slick bun, and thick glasses.

"You made it."

That snapped Doe out of her trance.

"Yeah, sorry we're late," I said. "I couldn't rush her, because I didn't want her to know what I was up to."

"That's totally okay." Kennedy smiled. "We're on your time."

"What's going on?" Doe asked, tugging my hand gently.

"I'll um... give you two some privacy," Kennedy offered. "When you're ready, I'll be in the room across the hall."

"Aight, cool." Turning my attention to Doe, I took her free hand into mine as she looked up at me with expectancy. "So... when we get back home, life will be different for us. Baby Boy will be here soon, and I was thinking we could end the babymoon by keeping the focus on just us."

Her cheeks lifted as she smiled and rocked from her toes to her heels. "What did you have in mind?" she asked sweetly.

"I was thinking we could get married. I already applied for the license. If you're down, all you have to do is sign. After we have our ceremony, Kennedy will mail it."

"And I'll be your wife?"

"Forever. And I'll be your husband." Her smile dropped

and eyes watered. For a second, I thought I'd done something wrong. "We don't have to get married today, sweetheart. We can wait an—"

"No, I..." Sniffling, she wiped a quickly fallen tear. "I'll marry you whenever, wherever. I'm just really surprised." With a giggle, she pulled me as close as her belly would allow. "Let's get married!"

Relief washed over me as I held her close. "Let's get married."

We released each other, then I let Kennedy know we were ready. She led us to our separate dressing rooms, and it wasn't until I was in mine alone that I realized the magnitude of this moment. When we left Rose Valley Hills, Dauterive would finally be my wife. All I could do was thank God that He didn't allow us to ruin His plans.

5

D auterive

EVERYTHING HAD BEEN TAKEN CARE OF, AND I DO MEAN everything. My hair and makeup, the dress, the shoes, and accessories... all thought out and executed by my man, with the help of my sister and parents. Even though this was our sacred moment, it made my heart glad to know they'd be able to watch via livestream. I had no idea Asylum had been planning a wedding for our babymoon, but it shouldn't have surprised me. He'd been dropping subtle hints all throughout my pregnancy about wanting us married before the baby came. It didn't matter to me. I knew regardless of when it happened that I'd be the mother of the rest of his children and his wife.

I couldn't stop staring at myself in the mirror. The white off-the-shoulder gown was the perfect fit. I loved how it molded against my breasts and stomach yet flowed freely against my lower half. My feet were bare underneath the long train. It was taking everything in me not to cry again because of how well everything had been put together.

Dallas had to be the one who selected my hairstyle because the feathered loose curls were perfect. The light knock on the door gained my attention. I told whoever it was to come inside.

"It's almost time," Mali announced. "You ready?"

"More than ready."

"Yay! Follow me."

She extended her hand for me, and I took it. I thought I'd be nervous on my wedding day, but I was so at peace. That was how I knew I was marrying the right man. A few steps later, we were standing in front of the exhibit that had a reserved sign in front of the doors. Unlike the rest of the exhibits with glass windows to see through, this one had black curtains hiding what was inside.

When Haley Reinhart's "Can't Help Falling in Love" began to play and the double doors opened, I saw why. Clutching my chest, I stopped breathing at the sight before me. Asylum stood in a sea of yellow and orange marigolds and sunflowers. It was the brightest, most beautiful sight I'd ever seen. He looked devilishly handsome in his white suit. There was something about my chocolate man in white with silver and platinum jewelry that made my pussy wet. Even today, that was the case.

The closer I got to him, the lighter he got on his feet. He kneeled as tears fell, and that moment was my undoing. I didn't bother wiping my tears as I laughed jovially. Once I made my way to him, Asylum hung his head and wrapped his arms around me. I pulled in a deep breath and thanked God for this man. A few seconds passed before he stood, wiping his face of its tears in this process.

"You look..." He chuckled as he looked me over. "You are the most beautiful being I've ever seen, Dauterive. I'm truly the most blessed man alive."

"Thank you, Asylum," I whispered, taking his hands into mine. "I love you so much, babe."

Cupping my chin, he tilted it and placed a sweet kiss to my lips. The sound of someone clearing their throat gained my attention. The officiant looked at us with a sweet smile as she said, "It's not time for that yet."

As I laughed, Sy said, "I'on really care about all'at. Just get me to the I dos."

That made me laugh harder because I knew he was serious. Still, she went through the usual spiel before asking us to say our vows and repeat after her. Finally, it came time for us to say 'I do' and slip on our rings. I think that was the moment where everything came full circle for me. A montage of our years together flashed across my mind as she pronounced us husband and wife, and every moment that we'd gone through, good and bad, I was grateful to God for... because I was *finally* Mrs. Dauterive Matthews.

Asylum
Four Days Later

THE DAY WE MADE IT BACK TO MEMPHIS, DOE'S WATER broke. Baby Boy said he'd waited long enough, and he was finally ready to come. Our family and friends waited at the hospital for his arrival. And twelve hours later... he'd come —all six pounds, nine ounces of him. I looked down at him as Doe held him in her arms. I could catch my tears in a bucket I'd cried so many. He was here, and he was healthy, and he was mine.

Mine.

The longer I stared at him, the louder I heard one word repeated in my spirit.

Peace.

Dauterive always said I was her safe haven. Her protector. Her peace. The man whose love drove her crazy yet kept her sane.

And she had always been and would always be my peace. My stabilizer.

Peace, for our son, seemed fitting.

"I got a name," I said.

Doe looked up at me with a tired smile. She'd never looked more beautiful than she did right now. I'd give my life for this woman, but more importantly, I'd fight to live forever to make sure she and our kids would always be straight.

"What is it?"

"Shiloh." She looked down at our son. "It means peace, tranquility, and abundance in Hebrew. It's the opposite of my name, but it's what we have always been to each other. What do you think?"

Doe gave him a kiss on his forehead. She sniffled and looked up at me with a smile as she fought her tears.

"Shiloh Amani Matthews. I think that's absolutely perfect, babe."

She gave him a second kiss before handing him to me. I wasted no time taking my baby boy into my arms. As I walked him over to the window, I smiled at the mirrored reflection of me that I held in my arms. It was boastful, but I wanted to make sure the angels had a better view of my prince. My thumb gently stroked his tiny chest as he rested against me.

"Shiloh Amani Matthews," I repeated, almost in disbelief. His little eyes fluttered before his dark brown orbs stared at me. "Daddy loves you," I whispered before kissing his forehead. "*So* fucking much."

Biting down on my bottom lip, I swallowed and held back my tears. I didn't think I would ever get to experience this—having a child who had my blood in their veins—and knowing he came from the woman that always had my heart made Shiloh's existence even more special. He was truly made with love, and I was going to make sure he, True, and Doe drowned in it for the rest of our days.

6

Merc

I WANTED TO TAKE THE PAIN AND DISCOMFORT FROM Neo. My girl had been in labor for hours and hours. We'd walked, she'd bounced on a big ass ball, and did compression presses. It was her doula, midwife, and me, and as calm and peaceful as they were keeping Neo... I was about to lose my shit.

Having a home birth was completely different from what I experienced with Aries and Marz at the hospital. This was more slowed down, hands on, and intimate. I loved being able to experience something so different with Neo since this was her first child and not mine. Doing it this way made us both experience a first. However, the downside to that was how nervous it made me. Regardless of how nervous I was, though, I kept on a brave, peaceful face. I didn't want Neo to feel my energy. She had enough to deal with.

"I'm going to get set up for a massage for Mama," her doula, Odyssey, told me. "Why don't you dance with her and keep her moving?"

"Sure thing," I agreed, helping Neo stand.

I'd been by her side the whole time—even when she didn't want me to be. There was no way in hell I was going to let her go through this alone. She didn't seem to be in as much pain right now, but she looked tired. I asked the midwife, Desha, to start the Al Green vinyl I had set up in the living room. As we swayed to the music, I asked Neo, "How you feelin', bae?"

"Exhausted," she answered quickly. "I'm ready for her to come."

Between the tears in her eyes and her whiney voice, I was ready to go up in that pussy and get my little girl.

"Is there anything I can do to make this easier for you?"

Neo gave me a smile, which was the first one she'd given since her water broke. "You being here is enough. I know I have to do this for us, but you being so present, patient, and loving is making all the difference in the world. I'm so scared, but I feel safe and a little ready to do this with you by my side."

"There's nowhere else I'd rather be. Thank you so much for carrying her and bringing her into this world, Neo. I'll forever be indebted to you for this." Her smile widened as I lowered to give her a quick kiss. "I love you, bae. The world is yours, I swear."

"I lo—hmm..."

Her frame bent, and she held her stomach, gripping my hand tightly.

"Breathe," Odyssey reminded. "Deep breaths, Mama."

I rubbed her back and held her hand until she was able to stand upright. When she was, she announced she needed a break from the dance. I laid her down on the couch since we'd set the living room up as her birthing room. I wished she could rest fully, but Desha was adamant about walking the baby down, so not too much time passed before she was back up and we were outside, taking a walk. I held her hand and cracked jokes, trying to make her smile. It seemed to work for a while.

When we got back to the house, I fed her frozen fruit bars to keep her hydrated because she couldn't keep water down. That made her cry and confess her love for me, which made me cry too. Then, it was time to walk again.

We alternated between massaging her and putting her in the little kiddie pool for hydrotherapy. At that point, I could tell her patience was starting to get a little thin.

"I'm ready for my baby," she almost whispered.

I was seated on the carpeted floor behind her, rubbing her stomach and kissing her neck. "Yeah?" I confirmed, starting to get a little excited.

"Mhm." She pulled in a deep breath and wrapped her arm around my neck from behind. "I-I feel like I need to push, Mercury."

"Aye!" I yelled, probably a little louder than was needed since Desha and Odyssey were in the room. "She said she needs to push."

They both held relaxed smiles as they walked over to us. My heart began to race as they shifted her from her butt to her feet. In a squatted position, they guided her through breath work and pushes. It was as if time sped up. Hours turned into minutes and seconds of me affirming her, kissing, and holding her, rubbing her arms and back... I was amazed, watching as my little girl entered the world.

25

"Oh shit!" I saw that black patch of hair and bounced from one foot to the other. "She comin', bae."

"Here." Desha reached for my hand, allowing me to feel the top of my little girl's head.

My eyes squeezed shut as I smiled. Neo whimpered before it turned into a groan.

"You got it, Neo. Keep breathing. You're doing such a good job," I coached, rubbing her back. "She's almost here. You're about to meet our baby girl."

A few pushes and deep breaths later, and she was out. I saturated Neo's face with kisses as Odyssey placed her on her chest. Her breathing was ragged, and she could barely keep her eyes open, but a smile was on her face.

Our little girl was finally here.

***

It wasn't until both of my girls were asleep that the weight of the moment finally settled on me. The midwife had checked their vitals and made sure they were good. We did skin to skin and made sure both Neo and our little girl were warm. After the cord was cut, I finally stepped out to get some fresh air, and that was when I broke down. Not just because she was here but because Neo had given birth like a fucking G. I'd never seen anything like it. She was so strong and calm, patient and steady... the shit blew my mind. To have been a part of it, I was just in awe.

I notified our people that Merci was here before going back inside. I freshened up and made sure I was good before either of them woke up and needed my attention. It wasn't long before our families and friends started to pull up. Our fathers wasted no time congratulating me with gifts and threatening me to never let my girls go without anything they needed. As anxious as everyone was to see them, I made it clear they had to wait until Neo was up to visits. I appreciated the fact that they weren't just hyper focused on the baby but wanted to visit with her too.

Our family room was just that—a family room, with all our people waiting on the chance to love on my girl and welcome our Merci into the world, and I was grateful to God for them all.

7

N eo
Three Months Later

I was sure all mothers said this, but I had the most beautiful, perfect baby. Merci was my pride and joy. She was my *whole* heart. I didn't think it was possible to love someone in such a small amount of time the way I loved her. I mean... true, her daddy and I fell for each other fast and deeply, but still. What I felt for my baby was to no end.

As I got her all comfy and cozy in her onesie, I looked down at her with a smile. The sight of her chubby cheeks and gummy smile was like an instant boost of oxytocin. I did the last button then picked her up and gave my baby kisses. Merci was the best part of me in human form—I was convinced. As happy as I was to be her mom, I still had some struggles.

I didn't feel like myself. My energy and libido were low.

I was happy to be a mom and loved my baby, but I also struggled with days filled with sadness. Merc and our families and friends were so helpful, and Odyssey too, but I still felt overwhelmed. Regardless of how much they did, Merci was *my* baby. She was most bonded with me. I wanted to make sure she felt as safe and secure as she possibly could because she was still so new to the world. She consumed my days and my life, and I was... simply... tired and overwhelmed.

Mama said I had the baby blues. Whatever it was, I wanted it to be over. I missed my man and wanted to experience him intimately. Hell, I missed myself. Merc and I hadn't been on a date or had sex since I gave birth. He was being so patient with me, which only made me feel worse. I prayed that I would be able to just... snap out of this... but that hadn't been the case.

There were times where I'd be good and then all of a sudden needed to be alone. I was often moody and not interested in any of the things that used to interest me, and my sleeping was horrible. I didn't know what the hell to do. Mama and Mrs. Nivea, Merc's mom, told me to give myself grace, but I felt like I was failing. Mrs. Nivea assured me that it could take up to two years for me to start feeling like myself again.

How would I endure two years of this?

I took Merci into the kitchen so I could grab a snack. I didn't have an appetite but knew I needed to eat. Merc hired a newborn care specialist, personal chef, and housekeeper for us. I wasn't going to my store or doing anything other than resting and taking care of Merci, which may have been a part of the issue too. He was trying to make sure I was comfortable, which I appreciated, but I felt like I'd lost myself.

After grabbing my bell peppers that were stuffed with cream cheese and bacon and topped with Everything Bagel seasoning from the refrigerator, I went to our bedroom and got Merci set up in bed next to me. As I snacked, I scrolled social media and enjoyed the moment of peace. It wasn't long after that before Merc was coming home. I was happy he was here and hoped my emotions would stay locked in to that. Our NCS would be arriving in a few hours, so he was more than likely going to love on us both until she got here then get some rest.

The moment my eyes landed on him, they watered as I smiled. I thought after I gave birth, I'd be the happiest woman alive. I thought things would be perfect. And even though I was happy, not having control over my shifting energy and emotions made me feel so shifty and unreliable.

"Hey, babe." I greeted him as he walked over to us wearing a smile of his own. He'd been working to open his training center, and I was so proud of him for that.

"Hey, beautiful." He graced my lips with three kisses before kissing my forehead. "I missed you today. How y'all been?"

"Good."

He made his way to Merci and picked her up, looking at her in awe. I'd never deny his partnership and love for our little family.

"You want me to take her so you can have a break?" he offered, more for his benefit than mine.

"Sure."

I felt my smile drop, so I looked away.

"What's wrong, bae?"

"Nothing."

"Do you want her?"

My head shook. "No, it's not that."

"You want me?" Smiling, I shook my head.

"No. Yes. I don't know, Merc. Maybe I just need some fresh air."

Merc took my hand into his and led me out of our bedroom. After getting Merci secured in her crib, he grabbed her monitor, and we went out onto the patio. It was mid-April, not too cool or warm. Before I could sit on the chair next to his, he was grabbing me and setting me on his lap. As his arms wrapped around me, he kissed my neck.

"I'm here." My eyes watered and closed at his declaration. Gritting my teeth, I swallowed hard. "Tell me what to do to help you."

"I don't know," I replied honestly. "I just feel like a bad partner."

"Why?"

"We haven't had sex or gone out on a date. I feel like I've let myself go." Sniffling, I wiped my face. "My moods and energy all over the place." Huffing, I turned slightly and looked at him. "I love Merci and Marz, and I love the family we've built, but... I don't know. I just feel like I'm losing myself. I feel like I'm letting you down."

His hand wrapped around the back of my neck, and he pulled me forward, kissing all over my face. The gesture made me smile like it always did.

"You had a baby three months ago. You're allowed to not feel like yourself. You're not failing me, and you are an *amazing* partner. I don't care that we aren't having sex and going out."

"But I do. We used to go out faithfully and have so much fun. Now I don't have the energy to do hardly anything."

"It's not like that's intentional, bae. Give yourself some grace."

"I'm trying," I muttered. "I just feel bad. We've been cleared for sex, and I can't get in the mood. How am I going to give you another baby any time soon?"

With a chuckle, Merc took my hands into his.

"I know we agreed to have three kids, back-to-back, to get it out the way, but we don't have to. At all. I'm content with the two we have. You're more to me than pussy and a womb. You're my best friend and life partner, and I love you. I don't care what we do or don't do. I just want you to be happy and at peace."

That made it impossible for me to hold my tears back. Cuddling against his chest, I continued to talk to him about how I felt, which was a first. Up until now, I didn't want to burden him with my feelings. He had been so helpful and such a great man and father. Now I regretted waiting so long to be honest with him about how I felt.

8

M^{erc} Six Weeks Later

IT WASN'T THE BABY BLUES. THAT DIDN'T LAST AS LONG as what Neo was suffering with lasted. She had a very mild case of postpartum depression, but it was postpartum depression, nonetheless. They got her on a medication that she agreed to take only for thirty to sixty days, and she was set up with a therapist who suggested time with friends and family, along with me, but also time with herself doing the things she once loved.

Neo spent time enjoying live music, doing embroidery, and playing the piano when she was alone. That combined with time with me and others, along with the medicine and finally resting, helped.

When she finally started to look and feel like herself, I put together a trip for us to Bali. Her energy had been slightly back to normal, which made me confident that she'd be able to take and bounce back from a trip across the world. We'd been going on dates now, but we still hadn't had sex, which I was cool with. I knew how to jack my shit when I needed the release, and she didn't mind giving me hand or head regularly.

It fucked with me that she felt like she wasn't being a good partner. More than anything, that was what I wanted to correct. I knew I could tell her over and over again that I didn't care about what she was unable to do, but Neo wouldn't care until she was able to, so it was my prayer this trip changed that. As much as we would miss Marz and Merci, it was important to me that we have this time away to spend with each other. If my baby wanted us to reconnect so she could feel more like my partner, then that was what we were going to do.

It didn't take long to realize I made the right call bringing Neo to Bali. The moment we made it to the resort, a wide grin spread her lips. She took my hand into hers as excitement caused her to shimmy.

"This is so beautiful, Mercury. Ah! I can't believe we're really here."

"Anything for you. You know that."

I shot her a wink that made her blush before giving her a kiss. When she moaned against my lips, my dick started to get hard, so I pulled away. I got us checked in, and we were led to our family suite, which massive. I think my favorite part of the suite was the Jacuzzi with a view of the tropical valley.

"What should we do first?" she asked.

"Well... you have a day of self-care planned. Tomorrow and the next day, it's all about us."

Her arms wrapped around me. "Have I told you how much I love, respect, and appreciate you today?"

"You have." I gave her a kiss. "Have I told you how much I love, respect, and appreciate you today?"

"Yes, and this trip is showing me too. I don't know if I would have made it through this without you." Her eyes watered and she nibbled her cheek. "Thank you for being so good to me and our babies, Mercury. You've made this easier for me to work my way through, and I'll forever be grateful to you for that."

"Don't put me in my feelings before you leave now."

Her laughter made me smile. I loved hearing it more often now.

"It's the truth. Merci is the best gift God has ever given me. I've never questioned that. But you?" Her head shook as she put a little space between us and eyed me. "God broke the mold after He made you. I've never known a man like you, and I'm grateful to have you in my life. You're more than a gift; you're my treasure."

"Mm." Her words hit me in my head and heart. "You're *my* treasure, baby. You gave so much of yourself to get our baby girl here. Romantic love aside, you went to war with your heart and mind, and you're winning. Trust me when I say I cherish you, and there's nothing I won't ever do for you. I'm so in love with you, and I'm going to worship you for the rest of our days. Only God is topping you with me." As Neo licked her lips, she slipped my hand into her panties. "Ooh."

"I haven't been like this since I had her. Feel what your love and words... your actions... feel what you do to me, Merc."

"Shit, bae. You wet as *fuck*." My free arm wrapped around her as I slipped my fingers between her slippery folds. Her head flung back—eyes closed and mouth slightly open. "She wakin' up for daddy, huh?"

"Mhm." Biting down on her bottom lip, Neo returned her eyes to mine as I circled her clit.

"Yeah, she takin' this dick while we here." It was taking everything inside of me not to slip my fingers into her pussy, but I wanted my dick to feel her walls first because it had been so long. So I continued to work her clit and opening until she came and trembled as she clung to me. Pulling my fingers out of her sweats, I licked her cum off each one.

My baby was back.

9

eo

THESE TEARS WERE HAPPY TEARS. I'D SPENT THE DAY AT
the Pyramids of Chi. Between the breath work, sound bath
healing, meditation, and the Harmonise and Energise
session, I felt like a new woman by the time I left. I couldn't
stop smiling and releasing happy tears. Originally, I didn't
want to take any medication, but I couldn't lie and say the
medicine along with my tribe and resting had not been
working wonders for me. But this time with Merc in Bali
felt like the final piece that had been missing. I felt more
like myself than I had since before giving birth, and I was
grateful to God for that.

After wiping away my tears, I did my skincare routine
and headed out of the bathroom. Merc was looking edible,
lying in bed in nothing but his boxers. His eyes were closed,
and he looked relaxed, but I was hoping he didn't plan on

going to sleep any time soon. My pussy had been unlocked, and she was desperate to welcome him back in. As I climbed into the king-sized bed, he opened his eyes and looked at me with a smile.

"You look like you," he said as I straddled him. "There go my baby."

Pride filled me as I pulled him up for a hug. That hug turned into kissing. That kissing turned into me grinding against him. His hand slid between us, and my legs locked around him. The seat of my panties was soaking wet, and I'd *just* put them on.

He pushed them to the side, and a low groan escaped him.

"I'm ready." A hiss escaped me as he slid his fingers against my opening.

"Are you sure, Neo?"

"Yesss."

Holding me by my waist, he lifted me, and I pulled him out of his boxers. Sitting down on him slowly, I held my breath until he was all the way inside. I think we both were too in need of this moment to give a damn about oral or extensive foreplay. I hadn't felt whole like this in months, and it was just what I needed.

Him in me.

His lips on mine.

Hands gripping my waist.

Breath on my neck.

Moans in my ear.

God.

I needed this. I needed him. Always needed him. Only needed him. Whatever... just *him*.

I was... embarrassingly wet. The stickiness of our thighs connected each time I bounced against him. As my walls clenched and pulsed, my nails dug into his head and shoulder as I came and held him close.

"Get up, bae. I'm 'bout to cum."

The second his dick popped out of me, his seeds erupted. His moan trembled as he jerked and tugged his bottom lip between his teeth. I loved the sight of this man in every form, but this... this was one of my favorites. Merc slipped back inside and switched our positions, laying me on my back.

For a while, he just stared at me. I'd been my most vulnerable with this man, yet there was something about the pure love in his eyes as he looked at me that made me shy.

"I missed you. Thank you for coming back to me."

Blinking back my tears, I lowered him to me for a kiss. "Thank you for being patient with me. I love you so much, Mercury."

"I love you more."

He pulled out and made his way between my legs, slowly licking and slurping my clit until he pulled another orgasm out of me. My clit was so sensitive I couldn't stop my legs from shaking.

"You good?" he asked with a chuckle.

"Yes, babe," I replied, putting his head back between my legs.

His fingers slipped inside of me as he continued to feast on my pussy, not stopping until I came again and couldn't take anymore. Merc pressed his way back inside and connected his lips with mine, making love to me for the rest of the evening.

Two Days Later

. . .

"Fuck!"

Merc released a sizzling breath as he gripped my hair. It was our last full day in Bali, and I wanted to wake him up right. As his dick tapped the back of my throat, I looked into his sleepy eyes.

"Mm... you sucking the shit out of my dick, bae. Damn."

As my hand worked the base of his shaft, I ran my tongue down his length before closing my mouth around him. The combination of sucking and wrist work was always his undoing. It wasn't long before he was cumming and shooting his seeds down my throat.

Making my way up his frame, I gave him a sloppy kiss before lifting his shirt from my body. He wasted no time taking each of my nipples into his mouth.

"Good morning," I said with a giggle.

"It's a very good morning. Bend that ass over."

Assuming the position, I got on my knees and forearms, arching my back in preparation. Merc smacked both ass cheeks before spreading them and slipping inside of me. I couldn't stop myself from moaning even if I tried. I felt him all over me. He started slow and steady, rocking me against him and allowing me to match his pace. When my toes started to tingle and wetness began to coat him, he picked up the pace. His strokes were so hard and deep, all I could do was hum and whimper as I savored each one.

"You take this dick so well," he complimented, voice sexy and shaky.

"It's so good. So good."

Merc spread my legs a bit more and pulled my hair, arching my back further. It didn't take long before I was cumming against him. He leaned back, allowing me to sit up and ride him in reverse. With his right hand massaging my clit and the left wrapped around my neck, Merc moaned and whispered in my ear about how good I was riding his dick.

"You gon' take this nut, huh?"

"I want every drop."

I continued to ride him until he was quickly pushing me forward and cumming on my ass. *"Fuuuck."* He grunted, tapping his dick against my ass. "You almost got pregnant again. I'ma have to get some condoms. It ain't safe tryna pull out of you."

I laughed as I plopped down onto the bed. A moan escaped me as he slipped back inside.

"You can cum in me, babe. We agreed…"

"Nah." He gave me one slow, long stroke that had me crying out instantly. "I don't care if we have to wait two or twenty years; I want you to get back to you before we do this again. I can wait, Neo."

"A-are you sure?" I moaned as he filled me again. "I don't mind getting our babies out the way, especially now that I feel more equipped to handle it, and my doctor said there's a chance I won't have it with the second and third baby."

He pushed my hair off my cheek and lay on top of me, but he didn't put his full weight against me. "I don't want to make a decision like that. It's yours. I know we agreed we'd have the kids a year or two apart, but I'm scared, bae. I don't want you to have to go through this again. If you're willing to risk it, you know I'll be with you every step of the way."

"How about we make no plans and just go with the flow? If it happens, it happens. If it doesn't, it won't."

"Okay, I can rock with that."

Merc gripped my ass and circled his hips against me, causing me to whimper.

"God, you're so deep."

"There's nowhere else I'd rather be."

My eyes rolled into the back of my head when he rocked against me again. "Shit, babe. You're about to make me cum again."

"Good. It ain't yours anyway. It's mine."

"Mercury," I moaned, gripping his wrist and trying to get back on my knees, but he wouldn't let me.

"Let me have it," he commanded against my ear, and I had no choice but to give him his cum.

10

Merc

I couldn't wait to get home to our babies, but I loved every moment of our time here. I loved cycling, sunrise hiking, and chasing waterfalls. Bali was probably the most beautiful place I'd ever visited. The resort itself was beautiful too. So beautiful we both decided we wanted to get married here in the future. I was able to get us an appointment to view the three places they offered as wedding venues—the bamboo nest, pool lawn, and wedding lawn.

The bamboo nest was just that—a cocoon like open structure that had a beautiful view of trees and the river valley. The pool lawn was like a large garden, and the wedding lawn was basically the same thing but bigger.

"Which one do you like most?" I asked Neo as we walked hand in hand along the grounds.

We had a packed day before heading home. We were going to go to the spa for foot baths, facials, and hot stone massages, before ending our day with a few laps in the heated infinity pool then floating dinner at the lower pool.

"I like the bamboo nest most. What about you?"

"Same," I replied.

"It's the most unique."

"Then I'll email the coordinator and let her know we'll book it when we get back home."

She squealed and hugged me. "Are we really going to come back here and get married? God, this place is like a paradise."

"We are, and it is." I wrapped my arms around her and placed a tender kiss to her lips. "Whenever you want, with whoever you want. That day will be yours."

"No, no. It'll be ours. Yours and our babies too. I want Merci to at least be able to walk. She might not be able to be the flower girl, but I want her to be here with us too."

"I agree."

"Ooh! I saw a video of a ballerina flower girl. That was pretty dope. Maybe we can do that. And of course Marz will be the ring bearer. What do you think?"

Chuckling, I lowered my hands to her ass and gave it a squeeze. I knew she wanted me involved, but I genuinely didn't give a fuck. I was just going to show up and claim her as my wife. None of that other shit mattered to me.

"That sounds perfect, Neo. So we're doing this after Merci is one?"

"Yeah, I think that'll be best." Her cheeks lifted as she smiled, but she covered her face and buried it in my chest. "Next year... we're coming here with those we love and getting married."

"Next year."

Her arms wrapped around me, and we both looked out into the valley. I wasn't sure how long we stood there, staring out into the beauty in the distance, but I'd never felt closer to God or Neo, and I'd never felt more at peace.

11

A snippet from Beethoven's upcoming book...

I t wasn't until we'd finished our steak and potatoes that Pops finally continued the conversation. I didn't know what else he could have wanted to say that required privacy, but I certainly wasn't expecting it to be, "I need you."

Out of my thirty-one years of life, my father had *never* uttered those words. In fact, I'd never heard him say he needed anyone. For as long as I could remember, he was always independent and the boss of all bosses. He didn't need anyone; people needed him—and that included my mother.

I didn't think they ever showed me a loving, healthy relationship. They showed me partnership and respect, but over the years, that faded away. My last year of high school, they divorced. Though my mother wanted me to live with her, I chose to stay with my father. We were closer, and as a man, I felt like it was more beneficial that I stay and continue to learn from him. While I wouldn't say I regretted that decision, not having my mother around to shield me from who my father truly was, showed me sides of him I didn't respect.

When it came down to business, I admired Tim Smith, boss of all bosses. As a father and a man, I resented him. Even with that resentment, I understood that was my issue and cross to bear, not his. He gave all he could and raised me as best as he could. Where he lacked, it was my responsibility to ensure I became a better version of him.

My mother and I were closer than ever. I respected her for staying with him as long as she did, but I was glad she was free to live as she pleased and be loved in a healthy relationship. Though she hadn't remarried, she'd been in a committed relationship with the same man for the last five years. Pops was married to the streets. He was passionate about this shit and didn't let anything come before it, not even his family.

"What do you need?"

Sitting back in his seat, he took a sip of his Old Fashioned.

"Your uncles and cousins are concerned. You know they always felt some type of way when it came to Robert. Envy. They hated that I let a non-Smith into the fold. Worse, he did better than them."

I nodded my agreement. That had never been a secret. Even though Pops was the boss of all bosses, he ran his organization like it was any other business corporation. He had a second in command, stand-ins on the off chance anything happened to him, lieutenants that worked directly with our men, and an advisory board that operated to make sure my father did what was best for the business as a whole, not just himself. So he may have made the final decisions when it came to things, but if at any point they felt like he could no longer run things successfully, they could have him removed.

I hated that he put the board in place, even if it was three of my uncles. I didn't like that anyone could take what he'd worked so hard to build. But that board gave his men more peace to trust his lead, and with the way they put their lives and freedom on the line for us daily, I guess that was all that mattered.

"What they tryna do? Keep you from putting someone in his place?"

"They want someone in the family to take his product monthly. I made it clear to them that none of them are capable of handling such a large amount. If we don't start to move that weight, they gon' start to feel the effect of it."

"And it won't affect your plate for quite some time. So I'm not sure why they are against what you planned to do."

"It's not that they're fully against it; they just want me to do it their way. They want me to keep Carlos out, and I can't agree with that."

"Aight, so what do you need me to do? Because I know if you don't fold, it'll be trouble with the lieutenants soon."

"Right. All it takes is for a few of them to question my authority and I'll have to go on a fuckin' killing spree." He sucked his teeth and sat up in his seat, crossing his arms on top of the table. "I don't have the time or desire to rebuild my leaders. That's where you come in."

I assumed he was going to say he wanted me to kill anyone who went against him and start anew. It wouldn't have been the first time I had blood on my hands after an order from my father, and I was sure it wouldn't be the last. I wasn't just his stand-in; I was his enforcer too. When I first started in the organization, I was on the streets and in the fields to learn the business. After about five years, I was able to advance and hadn't had to touch product to grow it or deal it since.

"You believe that keeping Carlos and Robert's team on is the best move financially?" I nodded. "And you agree that it'll be even better if we take over it completely?"

"I'on know about that, Pops." I sat up and looked around the restaurant, buying time while I tried to figure out how I wanted to say what I wanted to say. "It's not that I want to spare his life. I just feel like that's going to put a large weight on our shoulders. For the clientele Robert has, I'm not comfortable agreeing with taking over until after I've had time to see how his team moves and operates. If they can be trusted. If they will mesh with ours. The money would be good, but I need to know the risks will be worth it."

"I can respect that, and I also respect your honesty about it. That's why you're the only man I trust with this."

"With what, Pops? Just spit the shit out."

He chuckled and licked his lips. Usually, he was straight to the point.

"The way to keep the peace with the board and still hold on to Robert's organization is to bring his son in with marriage since they aren't blood. That way, they will be family."

"I would agree, but you don't have a daughter for him to marry. You tryna give him one of your nieces? How are you going to pull that off?"

The playful expression that remained on his face from his laughter was replaced with one of seriousness.

"I don't want a niece to marry Carlos; I want you to marry his sister."

The hearty laughter I released brought tears to my eyes. There was no way he was serious about this shit. I had no desire to get married, and I for damn sure wasn't going to get married to someone I didn't even know.

"You're joking, right?" I asked as the last of my laughter died down.

"No, son. I'm serious."

Our eyes remained locked for a while before I damn near yelled, "*Hell* nah."

"Bay..."

"Nah, Pops. Now it's a lot I'll do for you and the business, but this ain't it."

He chuckled and shook his head as his tongue rolled over his cheek. "You say that as if you have a choice." I sat back in my seat. "You know family is over everything, and at times, that includes ourselves. You know how much this organization means to me. To us. This is your future. Your legacy. If you do this, it will prove to me that I can trust you to lead my men when I retire. If you don't, I'll make sure what I have *never* touches your hand." Pops stood. "Now I'ma give you twenty-four hours to think on it, though I've already made the decision for you. You're going to marry her, get inside their organization, and learn how it runs. When you're confident you're ready to take over, kill Carlos. I don't care what you do with the girl." He made his way on the side of me and palmed my shoulder. "Be at my place tomorrow at six for dinner with them, and please, be on your best fucking behavior."

It didn't matter how in control I tried to remain of my emotions. Before I could stop myself, I was standing and knocking everything off the table. All eyes were on me, including Pops. With a grunt, he shook his head and smiled as he continued out of the restaurant.

Truth was, I knew there was nothing I could do to get out of this. I did want to take over eventually. I also was fully aware that family and this organization meant everything. If Pops believed this was the best way to keep Robert's business and please the board, there would be nothing I could do to get out of it. So as much as I hated the idea of marrying someone I didn't know, I left *At Steak* defeated, because that would soon be my future.

Preorder Here

12

A snippet from Bully's upcoming book...

This kind of shit didn't happen to men like me. When you came from the hood I did, you didn't get to live your dreams. You didn't get to marry the good girl. Shit, you didn't get to live past twenty. I'd not only gotten out the hood and made something of myself, but I met and fell in love with the perfect woman for me and had a beautiful baby girl in the process.

Surrounded by the men I loved and trusted, I prepared to make Innvy my wife. I didn't believe in love at first sight until I laid eyes on her. Maybe it wasn't love—maybe it was an innate need that connected me to her and told me she was the one. Regardless of what it was, I'd been locked in because of it and didn't plan on that changing any time soon.

When someone knocked on the door, I expected it to be the wedding planner coming to make sure we were good to go. My heart damn near dropped to my feet when PJ walked in. It was like seeing a ghost from my past. A past I wanted no one in this room, and for damn sure not Innvy, to be involved with. He gave me a crooked smile and bob of his head. I shifted through the bodies, seeing lips moving but not really hearing what anyone had to say.

"The fuck are you doing here?" I asked quietly once we were face-to-face.

"When Rocco granted your favor, he told you there would come a time that he'd call upon you to return it—"

"Not right now," I pleaded. "I'm about to get married."

"It was an offer you didn't refuse, in exchange for a favor you wouldn't be able to deny." PJ continued, massaging his chin. "He wants to see you. Now."

"You good?" Merc checked, making his way next to me.

"Yeah, brother. Everything is everything." Running my fingers down my mouth, I tried to contain the rage that was building within me. "I need to walk him out, but I'll be back."

Without waiting for PJ to follow, I headed out of the room. Once we were outside, I turned to face him.

"I need fifteen minutes," I said. "Fifteen minutes to marry my girl. Then I'll come."

PJ's head shook. "You got two to say goodbye."

"Fuck!" I swore through gritted teeth, punching the wall next to me.

As much as I hated agreeing, I didn't have a choice. If Rocco was requesting that favor, it wasn't an actual request. PJ was the calm before the storm. I couldn't risk anything happening to anyone in this banquet hall because of me. So as much as I didn't want to, I nodded my agreement and headed to Innvy's dressing room.

All I could do was pray she was understanding and gave

me grace instead of hating me for this. My angel didn't know about my past and the things I used to be into, and this wasn't the way I wanted her to find out. Still, I knocked on the door and decided to be as honest as I possibly could be without telling her details it would put her in danger to know...

The End
and...
The Beginning
If you preordered Beethoven's book, he's up next.

Made in the USA
Columbia, SC
02 July 2024